MOUSEKIN'S
THANKSGIVING

story and pictures by
EDNA MILLER

Simon and Schuster Books for Young Readers
Published by Simon & Schuster Inc., New York

For Debbie

Simon and Schuster Books for Young Readers
Simon & Schuster Building
1230 Avenue of the Americas
New York, New York 10020

Published by the Simon & Schuster Juvenile Division
SIMON AND SCHUSTER BOOKS FOR YOUNG READERS
is a trademark of Simon & Schuster Inc.
Manufactured in the United States of America

10 9 8 7 6 5 4 3 2 1

10 9 8 7 6 5 4 3 2 1 (Pbk)

Library of Congress Cataloging-in-Publication Data

Miller, Edna, 1920–
   Mousekin's Thanksgiving.

   Summary: Mousekin and his forest friends struggle to
survive the winter together with a wild turkey.
1. Mice—Juvenile fiction. [I. Mice—Fiction.   2. Turkeys—
Fiction.   3. Winter—Fiction] I. Title.
PZ10.3.M5817Mq   1988   [E]   88-4461
ISBN 0-671-66859-5 Pbk   0-671-66470-0

Mousekin was hungry when he woke in the night.
A cold November wind blew through the forest.
It lifted and scattered the leafy roof
that covered his home on the ground.

Mousekin peered from his tiny lined nest
to the bare swaying branches above.
He looked for owls that hover on air
or hawks that might have awakened,
as he had, hungry in the night.

Only the wind playing harp through the trees
met Mousekin's large silken ears,
and a sound far off in the forest,
(a sound he had never heard before),
a very soft "gobble–gobble."

When Mousekin was certain all was still,
he hopped from his nest on the ground.
He ran to the foot of a hickory tree
where a store of his food had been buried.

Mousekin stopped in his tracks at the tree.
He squeaked and squealed with anger.
His store of nuts, seeds, and berries
had been stolen—*every one!*

The ground around was stripped and torn
down to the tangled roots of the tree.
The little mouse trembled with rage and fear.
No seed-eating creature he had known
could dig so wide and deep a hole.

Mousekin leaped for safety
and raced to the top of the tree.
He huddled there 'til daybreak.
When he dared to peer about,
he spied nutmeats, seeds, and berries
tucked into the tree's shaggy bark.

Mousekin was very hungry now.
He reached for one of the seeds.
Before he could pry it loose,
a woodpecker landed nearby.

"Be off!" he cried, as he went rat-a-tat-tat
with his beak on the hickory tree.
"I saw the creature that stole your food.
It was bigger than a pheasant.
It was bigger than a goose.
It was the biggest bird I've ever seen,
and it *might like mice!*"

Mousekin hurried to the bottom of the tree.
He was *very* hungry now.
A white-footed mouse makes certain
he has more than one winter's store.
He ran beneath the litter of leaves
that cover the forest floor,
'til he came to a tall evergreen.

Beneath the pine tree was a hole freshly dug,
where Mousekin had hidden another food store.
A pile of pine needles was all that was left
of weed seeds, beechnuts, and dried berries.

He heard the chatter of squirrels
as they woke in the tree above.
Mousekin knew squirrels ate nuts and seeds.

He squeaked and drummed his tiny paw
to let them know his anger.

"We didn't take your store of food,"
the frisky squirrels cried.
"Our food was gathered in the fall
and stored inside our nest."

"We saw the creature that stole your food.
It was very big and it was frightful.
It had a naked blue head and a warty red neck
with long sharp spurs on its legs."

More hungry than afraid,
Mousekin raced through the woods.
He had only one more store of food
to last the winter through.
It was hidden inside the stump of a tree,
in a tangle of leaves and brush.

When Mousekin reached his buried treasure,
he knew someone had been there before him.
The hollow stump was scratched clean of leaves
along with the last of his harvests.

Mousekin spied a cottontail napping in the brush.
Angrier than ever, he drummed his paw.
The rabbit woke and thumped her foot in answer.
"I didn't steal your winter store,
but I saw the one that did.
It was big. It was ugly.
And it made the strangest sound."

Not far from the stump in a stand of trees
they heard a "gobble–gobble."
The rabbit disappeared into her burrow.
Mousekin stood frozen with fear.

A huge bird rushed from cover.
His shining feathers
were ruffled and fluffed.
His wing tips made a rattling noise
as they brushed along the ground.

With tail feathers spread
like a great fan behind him,
he was a fearsome sight.

The wild turkey rushed past Mousekin.
He rushed at a swooping owl.
The owl had spied Mousekin
crouched in the clearing—
but quickly changed its mind.
It would never come that way again
to hunt for white-footed mice!

Mousekin scrambled to the top of a tree
and hopped inside a hollow.
He was still a very hungry mouse,
but glad to be alive.
As he fell asleep, he heard the turkey call,
"gobble–gobble–gobble."

As Mousekin slept,
the first snow of winter fell.
It blanketed the tops of the trees
and the forest floor below.
It hid the food all creatures need
to see a long, cold winter through.

Mousekin woke to the chatter of squirrels
and a woodpecker's rat-a-tat-tat.
He heard chickadees calling "chick-a-dee-dee,"
and the turkey's "gobble–gobble."

What Mousekin saw when he peered below
surprised the little mouse.
There was a happy gathering of creatures
and a feast spread out on the snow.

The wild turkey, with feathers unruffled,
dug beneath the deep white cover.
He turned up grapes, dried apples, and seeds.
There were acorns for everyone.

Mousekin scampered to the ground.
He stuffed his cheeks with all he could carry,
then hurried back to his nest in the hollow.

When evening came, Mousekin curled to sleep.
There would be plenty to eat and nothing to fear
with the big, friendly bird roosting near.